REBEL JAIL: VOLUME 4

It is a period of renewed hope for the Rebellion. Rebel heroes Luke Skywalker, Han Solo, and Princess Leia have captured Darth Vader's ally, droid expert Dr. Aphra, to obtain Imperial information.

While the Princess is securing Dr. Aphra at Sunspot Prison, an unknown attacker assumes control of the facility and begins eliminating the prisoners. Elsewhere, Luke and Han have taken a nerf smuggling job in order to regain the Alliance funds Han lost gambling.

Back at the prison, Leia and Sana Starros have forged an alliance with Dr. Aphra to take down the prison's mysterious invader – an enemy who may not be so mysterious after all....

JASON AARON	LEINIL FRANCIS YU	GERRY ALANGUILAN	SUNNY GHO	CHRIS ELIOPOULOS
Writer	Penciler	Inker	Colorist	Letterer

LEINIL YU & SUNNY GHO	HEATHER ANTOS	JORDAN D. WHITE
Cover Artists	Assistant Editor	Editor

C.B. CEBULSKI	AXEL ALONSO	JOE QUESADA	DAN BUCKLEY
Executive Editor	Editor In Chief	Chief Creative Officer	Publisher

For Lucasfilm:
Creative Director MICHAEL SIGLAIN
Senior Editor FRANK PARISI
Lucasfilm Story Group RAYNE ROBERTS, PABLO HIDALGO, LELAND CHEE, MATT MARTIN

ABDO
Spotlight

ABDOPUBLISHING.COM

Reinforced library bound edition published in 2018 by Spotlight,
a division of ABDO, PO Box 398166, Minneapolis, Minnesota 55439.
Spotlight produces high-quality reinforced library bound editions for
schools and libraries. Published by agreement with Marvel Characters, Inc.

Printed in the United States of America, North Mankato, Minnesota.
092017
012018

THIS BOOK CONTAINS
RECYCLED MATERIALS

marvelkids.com

STAR WARS © & TM 2018 LUCASFILM LTD.

PUBLISHER'S CATALOGING-IN-PUBLICATION DATA

Names: Aaron, Jason, author. | Mayhew, Mike; Yu, Leinil Francis; Alanguilan, Gerry;
 Gho, Sunny; Tartaglia, Java, illustrators.
Title: Rebel jail / writer: Jason Aaron ; art: Mike Mayhew; Leinil Francis Yu; Gerry
 Alanguilan; Sunny Gho; Java Tartaglia.
Description: Reinforced library bound edition. | Minneapolis, MN : Spotlight, 2018 |
 Series: Star Wars: Rebel jail | Volume 1 written by Jason Aaron ; illustrated by
 Mike Mayhew. | Volumes 2 and 4 written by Jason Aaron ; illustrated by Leinil
 Francis Yu; Gerry Alanguilan & Sunny Gho. | Volume 3 written by Jason Aaron ;
 illustrated by Leinil Francis Yu & Sunny Gho. | Volume 5 written by Jason Aaron ;
 illustrated by Leinil Francis Yu; Gerry Alanguilan; Sunny Gho & Java Tartaglia.
Summary: During Ben Kenobi's exile on Tatooine, he vows to keep a young Luke
 safe; Princess Leia and Sana Starros bring an important captive to the Sunspot
 Prison, where they are ambushed by a rebel spy on a mission of life and death;
 Luke Skywalker tries his hand at smuggling after Han loses their rebel funds in a
 gamble.
Identifiers: LCCN 2017941922 | ISBN 9781532141416 (volume 1) | ISBN
 9781532141423 (volume 2) | ISBN 9781532141430 (volume 3) | ISBN
 9781532141447 (volume 4) | ISBN 9781532141454 (volume 5)
Subjects: LCSH: Star Wars (film)--Juvenile fiction. | Adventure and Adventurers--
 Juvenile fiction. | Graphic Novels--Juvenile fiction.
Classification: DDC 741.5--dc23
LC record available at http://lccn.loc.gov/2017941922

Spotlight

A Division of ABDO
abdopublishing.com

STAR WARS™

REBEL JAIL

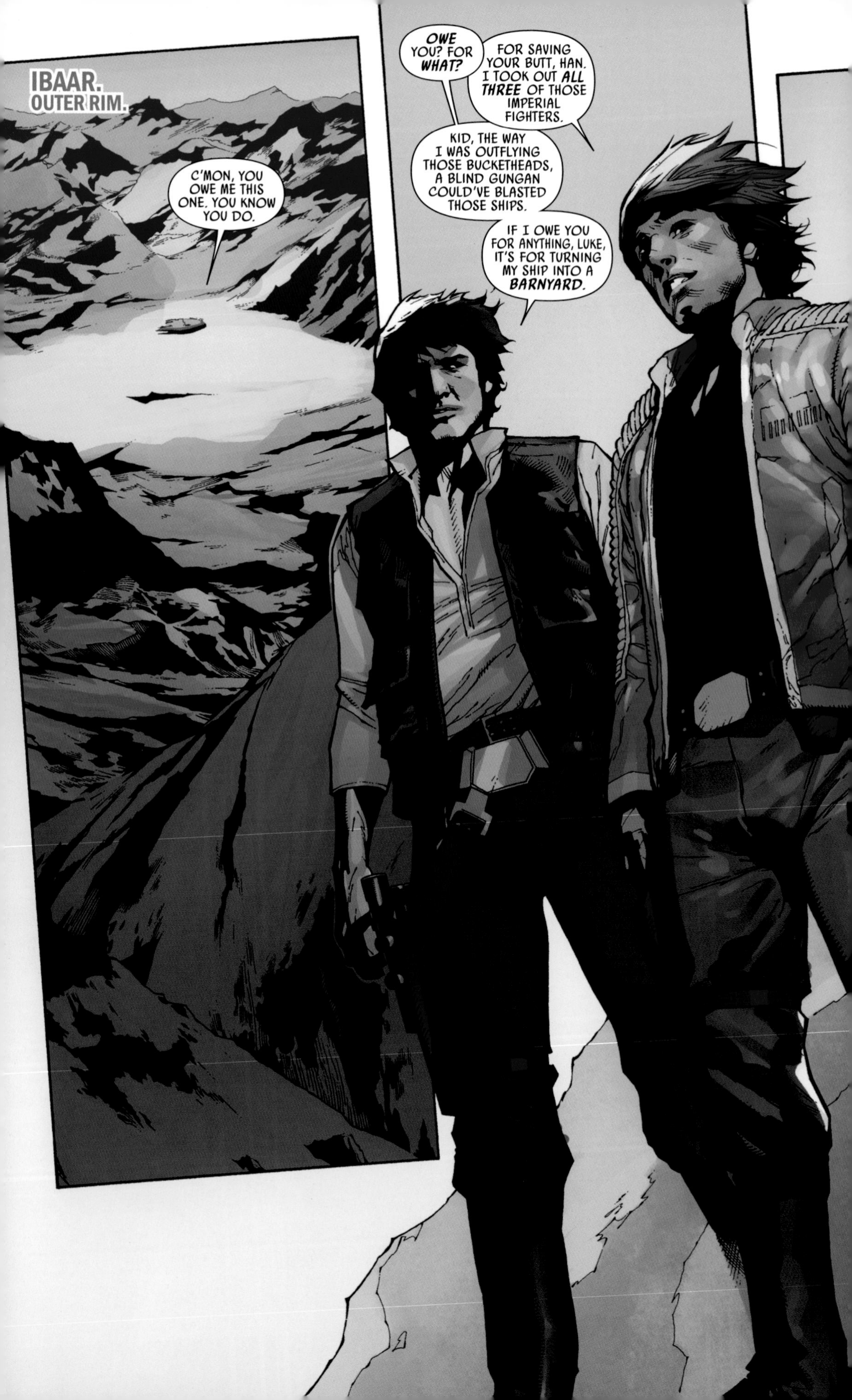
IBAAR. OUTER RIM.
C'MON, YOU OWE ME THIS ONE. YOU KNOW YOU DO.
OWE YOU? FOR WHAT?
FOR SAVING YOUR BUTT, HAN. I TOOK OUT ALL THREE OF THOSE IMPERIAL FIGHTERS.
KID, THE WAY I WAS OUTFLYING THOSE BUCKETHEADS, A BLIND GUNGAN COULD'VE BLASTED THOSE SHIPS.
IF I OWE YOU FOR ANYTHING, LUKE, IT'S FOR TURNING MY SHIP INTO A BARNYARD.

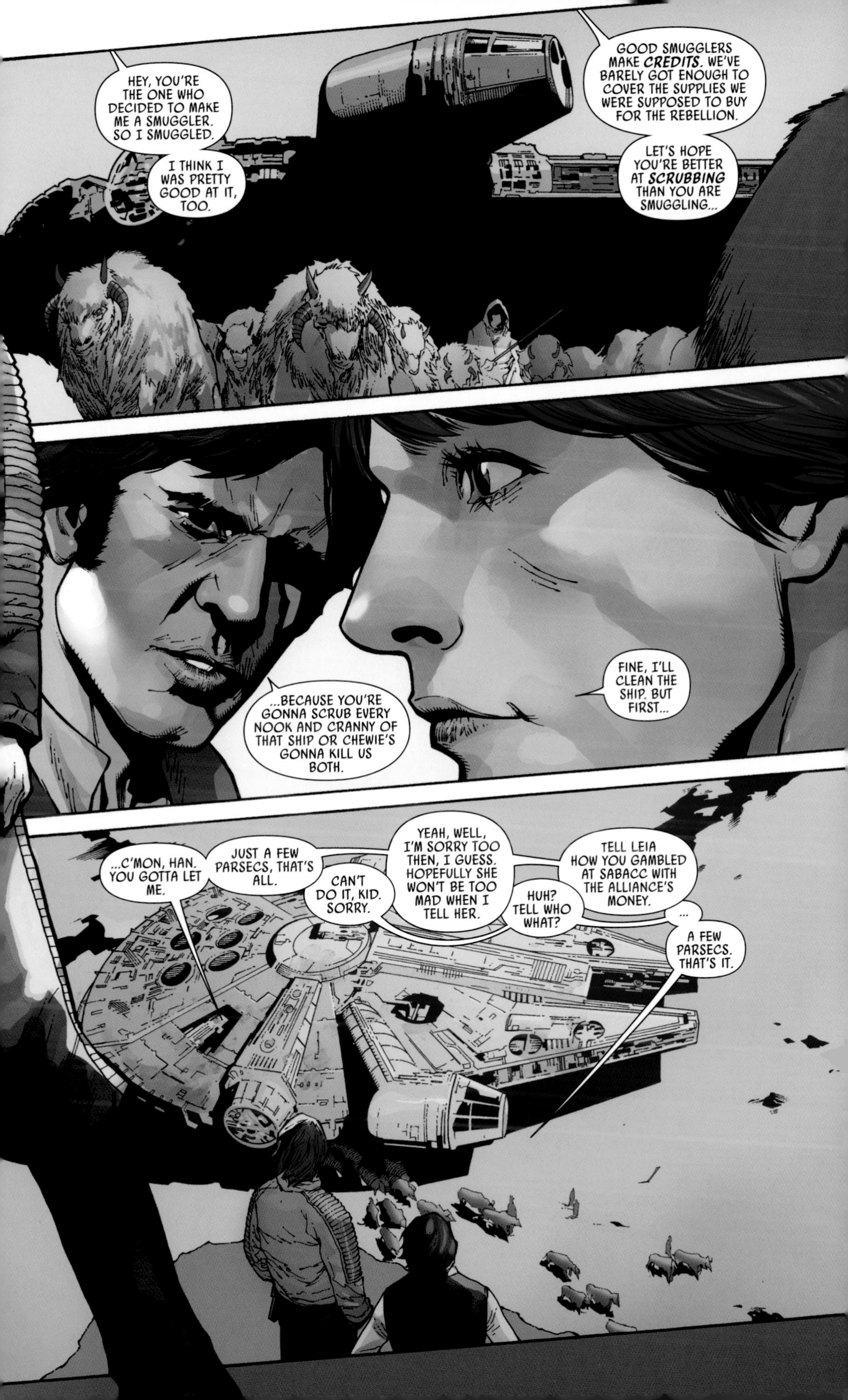
HEY, YOU'RE THE ONE WHO DECIDED TO MAKE ME A SMUGGLER. SO I SMUGGLED.
I THINK I WAS PRETTY GOOD AT IT, TOO.
GOOD SMUGGLERS MAKE CREDITS. WE'VE BARELY GOT ENOUGH TO COVER THE SUPPLIES WE WERE SUPPOSED TO BUY FOR THE REBELLION.
LET'S HOPE YOU'RE BETTER AT SCRUBBING THAN YOU ARE SMUGGLING...
...BECAUSE YOU'RE GONNA SCRUB EVERY NOOK AND CRANNY OF THAT SHIP OR CHEWIE'S GONNA KILL US BOTH.
FINE, I'LL CLEAN THE SHIP. BUT FIRST...
...C'MON, HAN. YOU GOTTA LET ME.
JUST A FEW PARSECS, THAT'S ALL.
CAN'T DO IT, KID. SORRY.
YEAH, WELL, I'M SORRY TOO THEN, I GUESS. HOPEFULLY SHE WON'T BE TOO MAD WHEN I TELL HER.
HUH? TELL WHO WHAT?
TELL LEIA HOW YOU GAMBLED AT SABACC WITH THE ALLIANCE'S MONEY.
...
A FEW PARSECS. THAT'S IT.

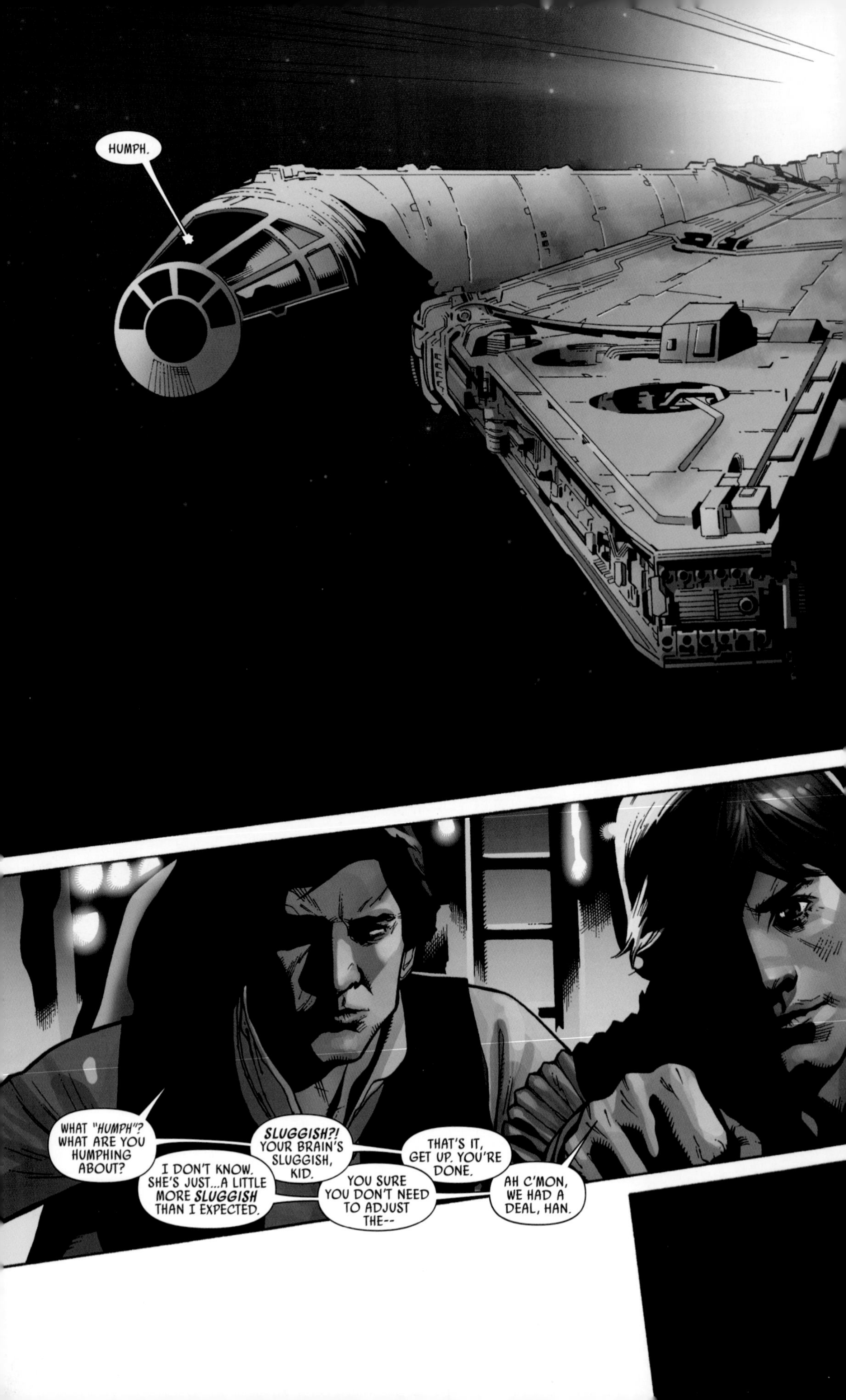
HUMPH.
WHAT "*HUMPH*"? WHAT ARE YOU HUMPHING ABOUT?
I DON'T KNOW. SHE'S JUST...A LITTLE MORE ***SLUGGISH*** THAN I EXPECTED.
SLUGGISH?! YOUR BRAIN'S SLUGGISH, KID.
YOU SURE YOU DON'T NEED TO ADJUST THE--
THAT'S IT, GET UP. YOU'RE DONE.
AH C'MON, WE HAD A DEAL, HAN.

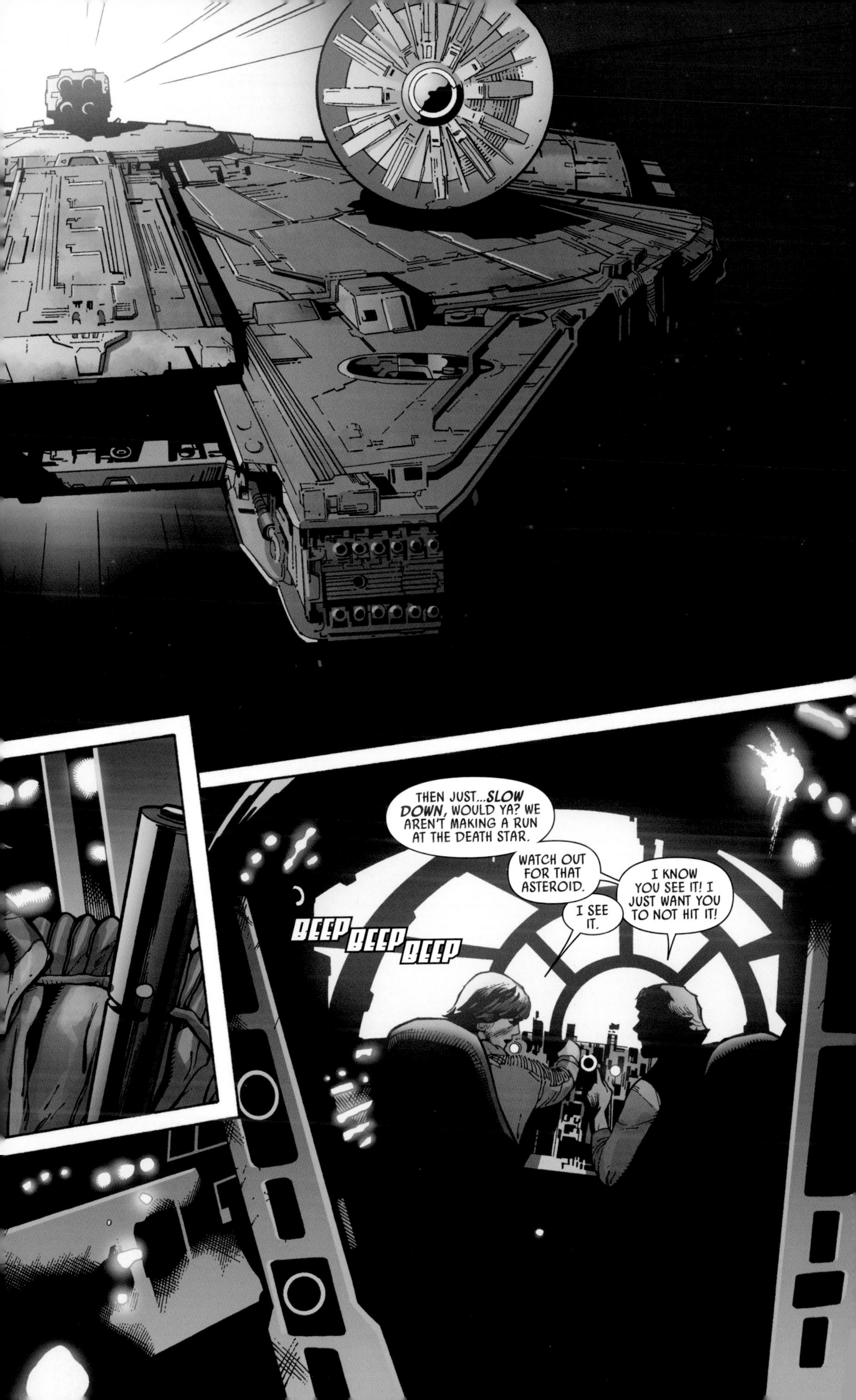
THEN JUST...SLOW DOWN, WOULD YA? WE AREN'T MAKING A RUN AT THE DEATH STAR.
WATCH OUT FOR THAT ASTEROID.
I SEE IT.
I KNOW YOU SEE IT! I JUST WANT YOU TO NOT HIT IT!
BEEP BEEP BEEP

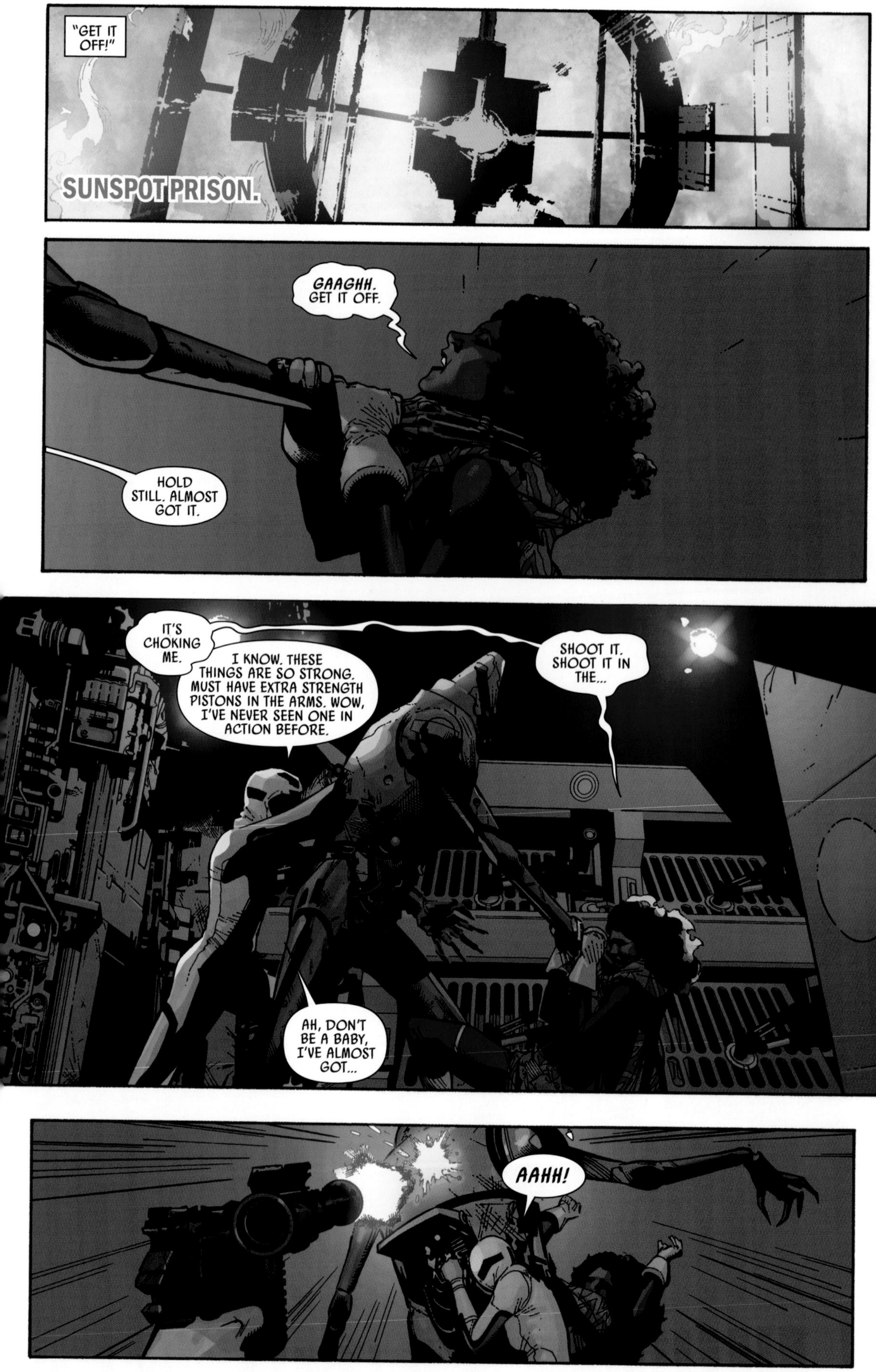
"GET IT OFF!"
SUNSPOT PRISON.
GAAGHH. GET IT OFF.
HOLD STILL. ALMOST GOT IT.
IT'S CHOKING ME.
I KNOW. THESE THINGS ARE SO STRONG. MUST HAVE EXTRA STRENGTH PISTONS IN THE ARMS. WOW, I'VE NEVER SEEN ONE IN ACTION BEFORE.
SHOOT IT. SHOOT IT IN THE...
AH, DON'T BE A BABY, I'VE ALMOST GOT...
AAHH!

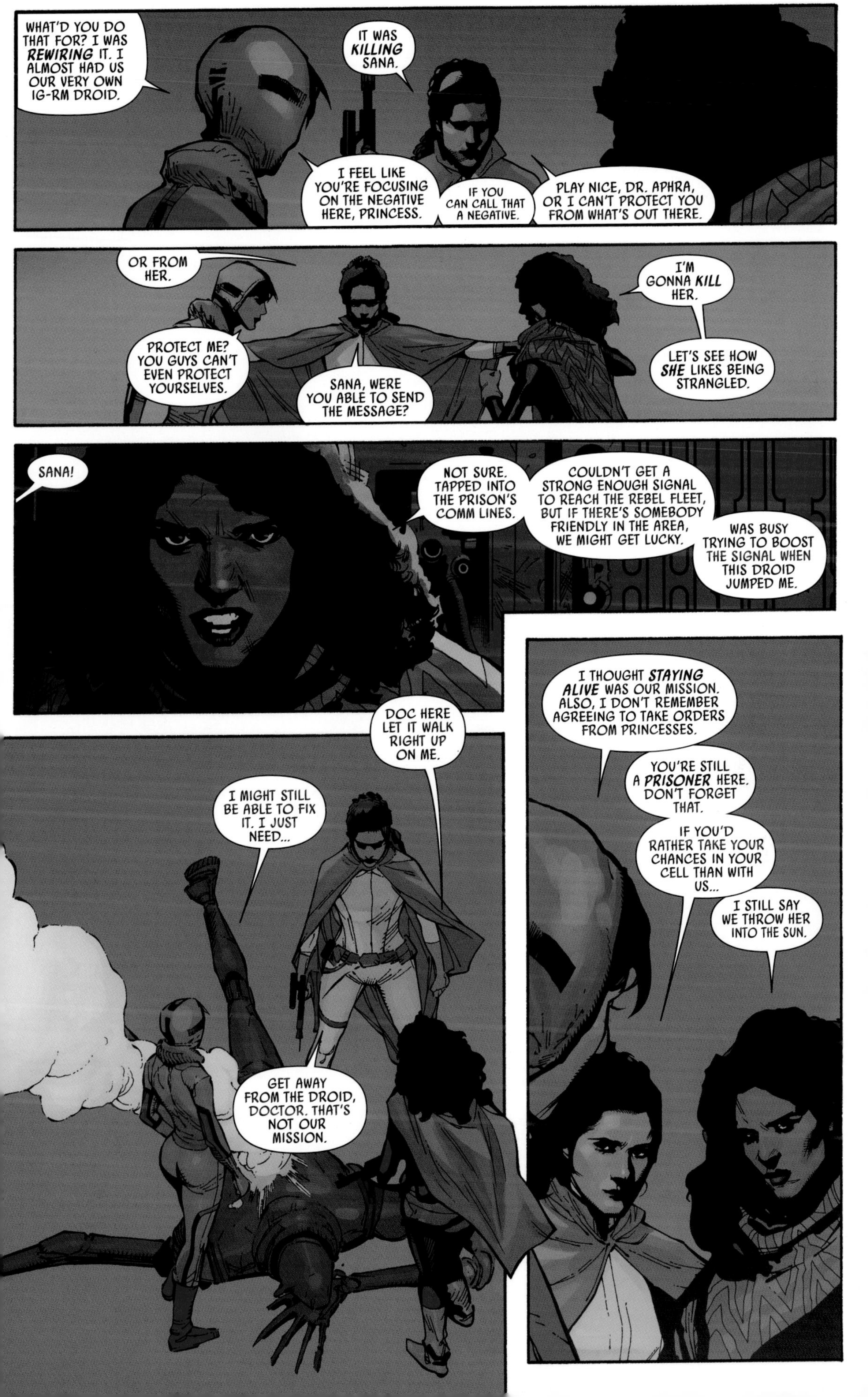
WHAT'D YOU DO THAT FOR? I WAS REWIRING IT. I ALMOST HAD US OUR VERY OWN IG-RM DROID.
IT WAS KILLING SANA.
I FEEL LIKE YOU'RE FOCUSING ON THE NEGATIVE HERE, PRINCESS.
IF YOU CAN CALL THAT A NEGATIVE.
PLAY NICE, DR. APHRA, OR I CAN'T PROTECT YOU FROM WHAT'S OUT THERE.
OR FROM HER.
I'M GONNA KILL HER.
LET'S SEE HOW SHE LIKES BEING STRANGLED.
PROTECT ME? YOU GUYS CAN'T EVEN PROTECT YOURSELVES.
SANA, WERE YOU ABLE TO SEND THE MESSAGE?
SANA!
NOT SURE. TAPPED INTO THE PRISON'S COMM LINES.
COULDN'T GET A STRONG ENOUGH SIGNAL TO REACH THE REBEL FLEET, BUT IF THERE'S SOMEBODY FRIENDLY IN THE AREA, WE MIGHT GET LUCKY.
WAS BUSY TRYING TO BOOST THE SIGNAL WHEN THIS DROID JUMPED ME.
DOC HERE LET IT WALK RIGHT UP ON ME.
I MIGHT STILL BE ABLE TO FIX IT. I JUST NEED...
GET AWAY FROM THE DROID, DOCTOR. THAT'S NOT OUR MISSION.
I THOUGHT STAYING ALIVE WAS OUR MISSION. ALSO, I DON'T REMEMBER AGREEING TO TAKE ORDERS FROM PRINCESSES.
YOU'RE STILL A PRISONER HERE. DON'T FORGET THAT.
IF YOU'D RATHER TAKE YOUR CHANCES IN YOUR CELL THAN WITH US...
I STILL SAY WE THROW HER INTO THE SUN.

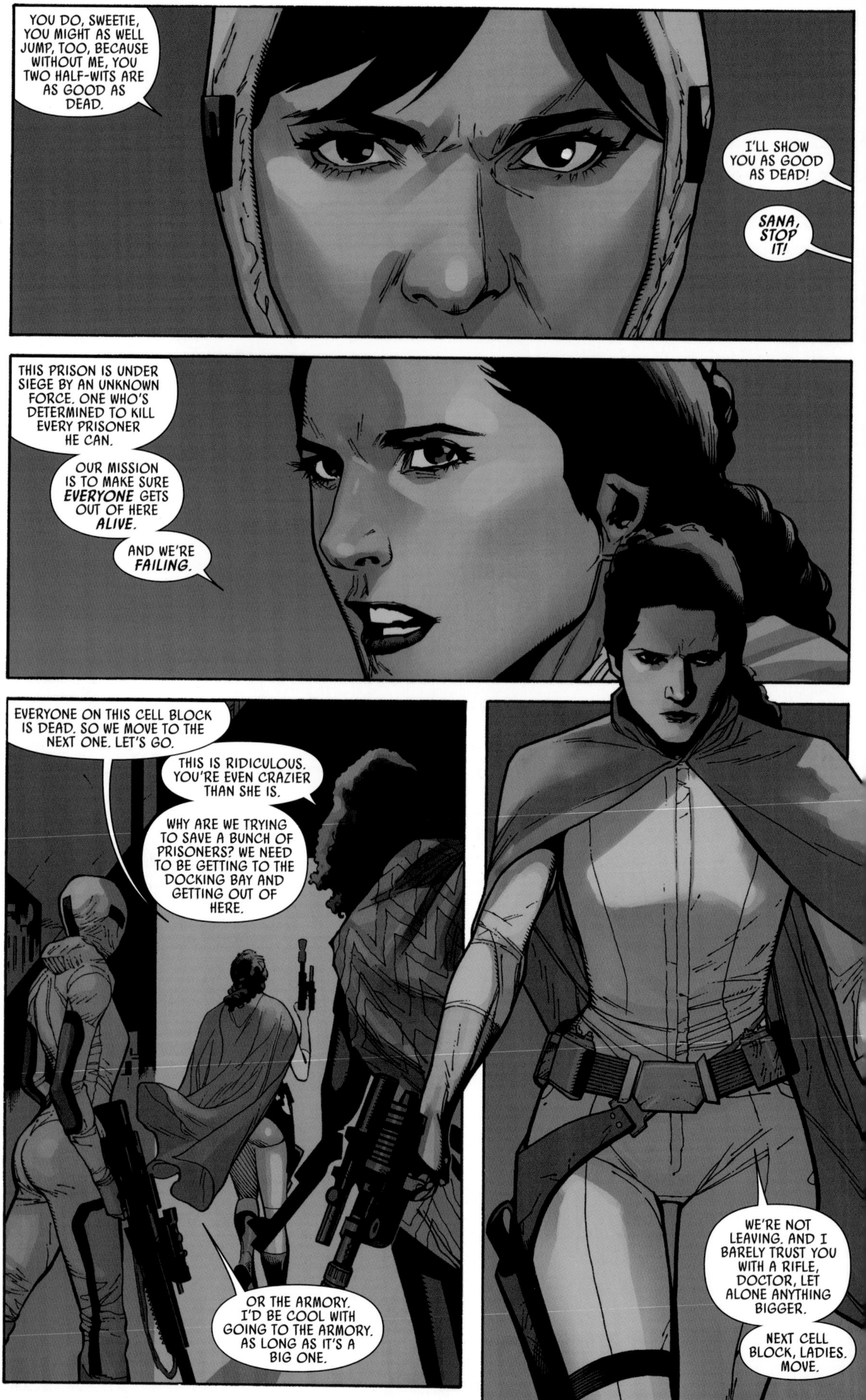
YOU DO, SWEETIE, YOU MIGHT AS WELL JUMP, TOO, BECAUSE WITHOUT ME, YOU TWO HALF-WITS ARE AS GOOD AS DEAD.
I'LL SHOW YOU AS GOOD AS DEAD!
SANA, STOP IT!
THIS PRISON IS UNDER SIEGE BY AN UNKNOWN FORCE. ONE WHO'S DETERMINED TO KILL EVERY PRISONER HE CAN.
OUR MISSION IS TO MAKE SURE EVERYONE GETS OUT OF HERE ALIVE.
AND WE'RE FAILING.
EVERYONE ON THIS CELL BLOCK IS DEAD. SO WE MOVE TO THE NEXT ONE. LET'S GO.
THIS IS RIDICULOUS. YOU'RE EVEN CRAZIER THAN SHE IS.
WHY ARE WE TRYING TO SAVE A BUNCH OF PRISONERS? WE NEED TO BE GETTING TO THE DOCKING BAY AND GETTING OUT OF HERE.
OR THE ARMORY. I'D BE COOL WITH GOING TO THE ARMORY. AS LONG AS IT'S A BIG ONE.
WE'RE NOT LEAVING. AND I BARELY TRUST YOU WITH A RIFLE, DOCTOR, LET ALONE ANYTHING BIGGER.
NEXT CELL BLOCK, LADIES. MOVE.

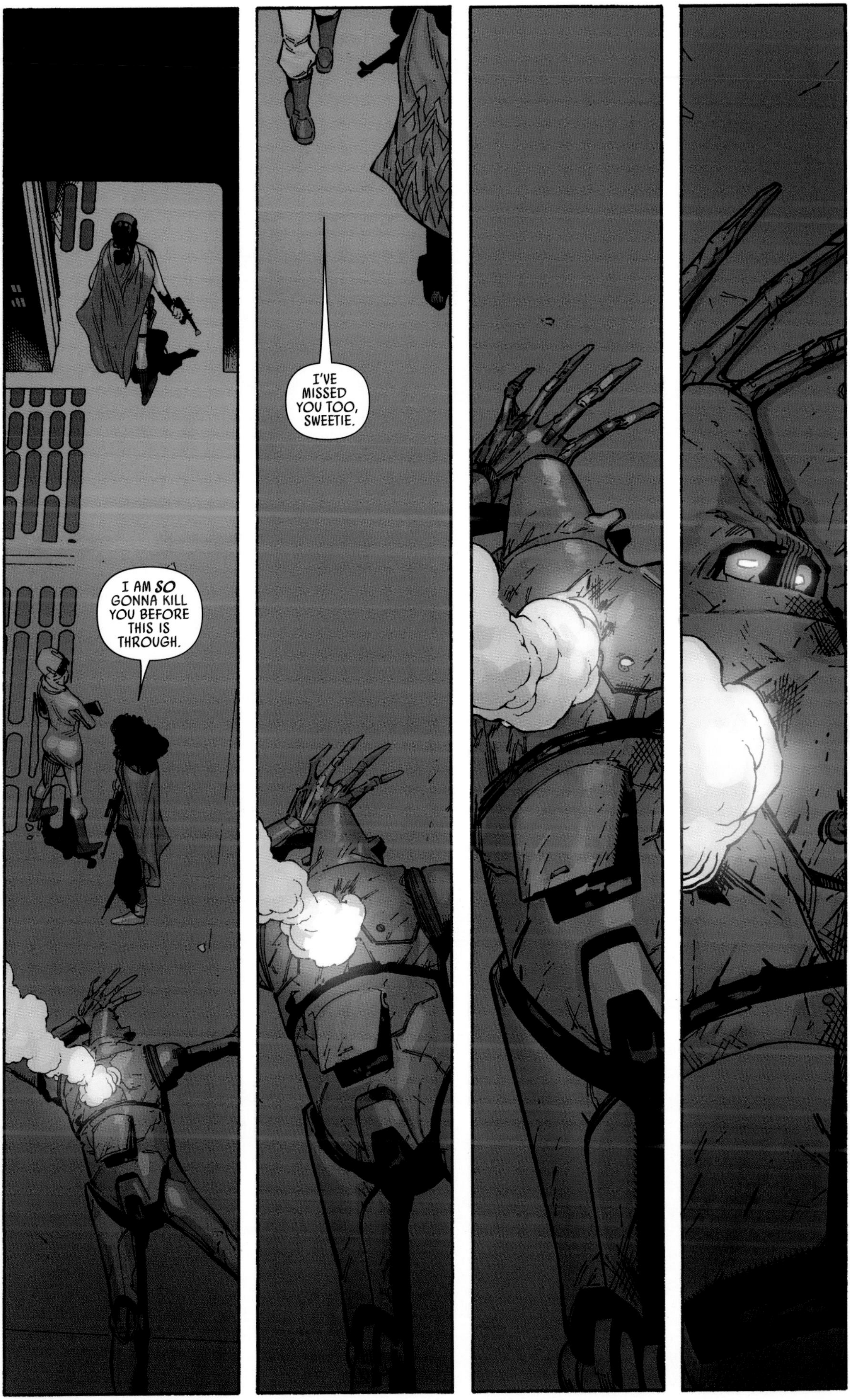
I AM SO GONNA KILL YOU BEFORE THIS IS THROUGH.
I'VE MISSED YOU TOO, SWEETIE.

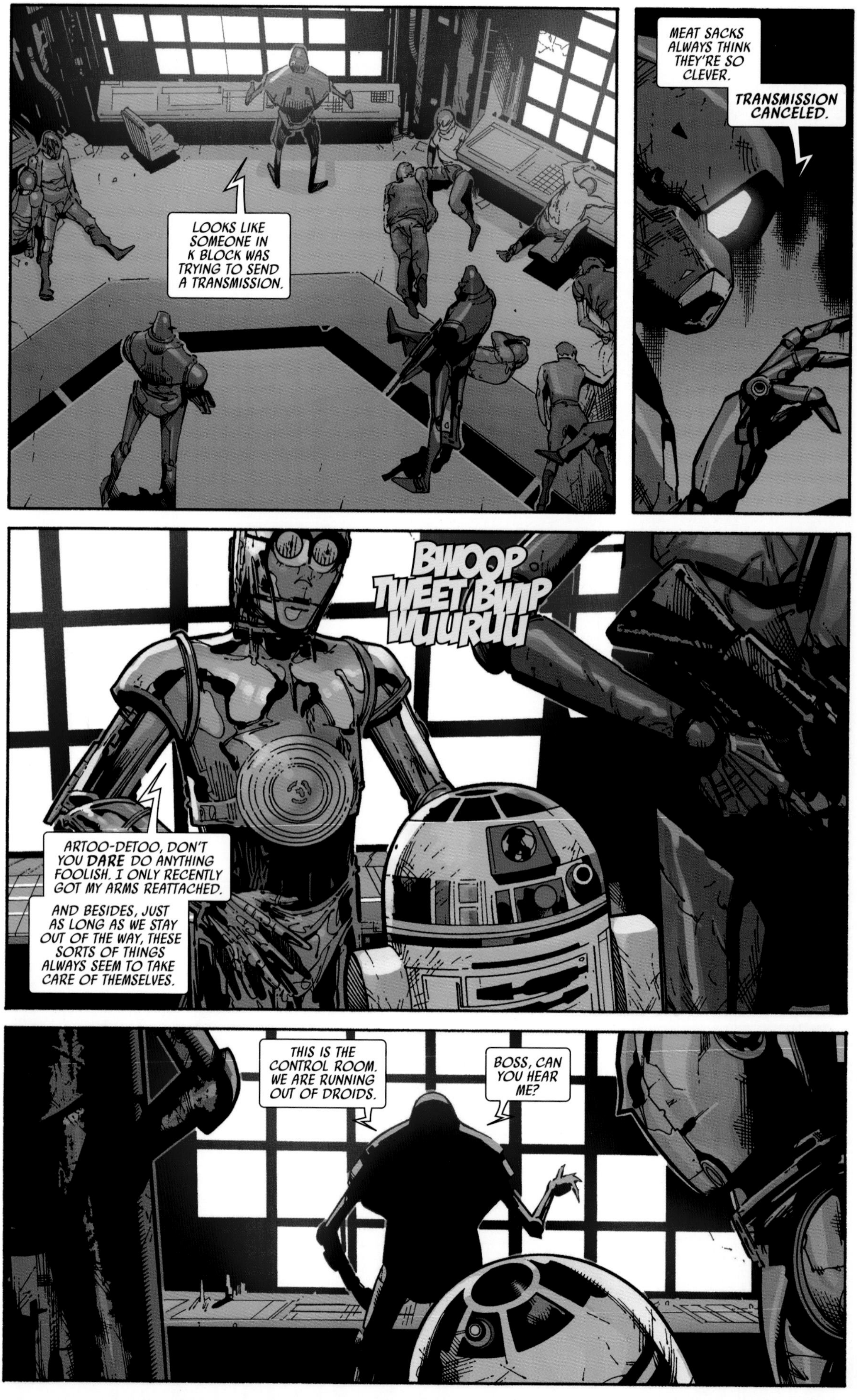
LOOKS LIKE SOMEONE IN K BLOCK WAS TRYING TO SEND A TRANSMISSION.
MEAT SACKS ALWAYS THINK THEY'RE SO CLEVER.
TRANSMISSION CANCELED.
BWOOP TWEET BWIP WUURUU
ARTOO-DETOO, DON'T YOU DARE DO ANYTHING FOOLISH. I ONLY RECENTLY GOT MY ARMS REATTACHED.
AND BESIDES, JUST AS LONG AS WE STAY OUT OF THE WAY, THESE SORTS OF THINGS ALWAYS SEEM TO TAKE CARE OF THEMSELVES.
THIS IS THE CONTROL ROOM. WE ARE RUNNING OUT OF DROIDS.
BOSS, CAN YOU HEAR ME?

BOSS?

OPEN CELL SEVENTEEN.

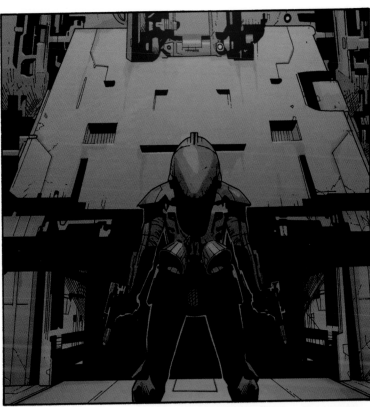

THEY KEPT YOU IN A *MAXIMUM SECURITY CELL.* THERE MUST BE A REASON FOR THAT.

TELL ME WHAT IT IS.

THREE REASONS.

THE THREE JEDI WHOSE THROATS I SLIT.

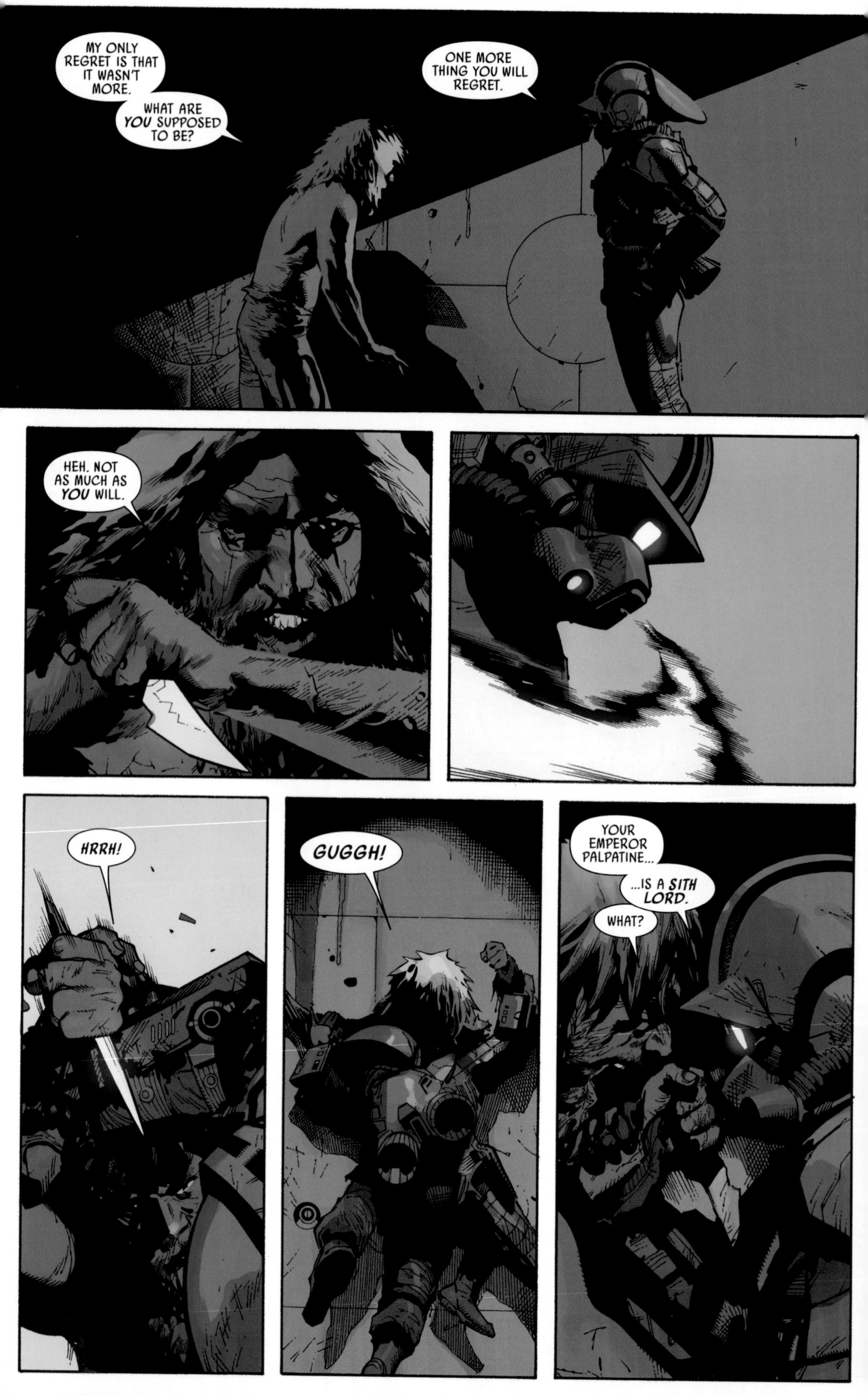
MY ONLY REGRET IS THAT IT WASN'T MORE.
WHAT ARE YOU SUPPOSED TO BE?
ONE MORE THING YOU WILL REGRET.
HEH. NOT AS MUCH AS YOU WILL.
HRRH!
GUGGH!
YOUR EMPEROR PALPATINE...
...IS A SITH LORD.
WHAT?

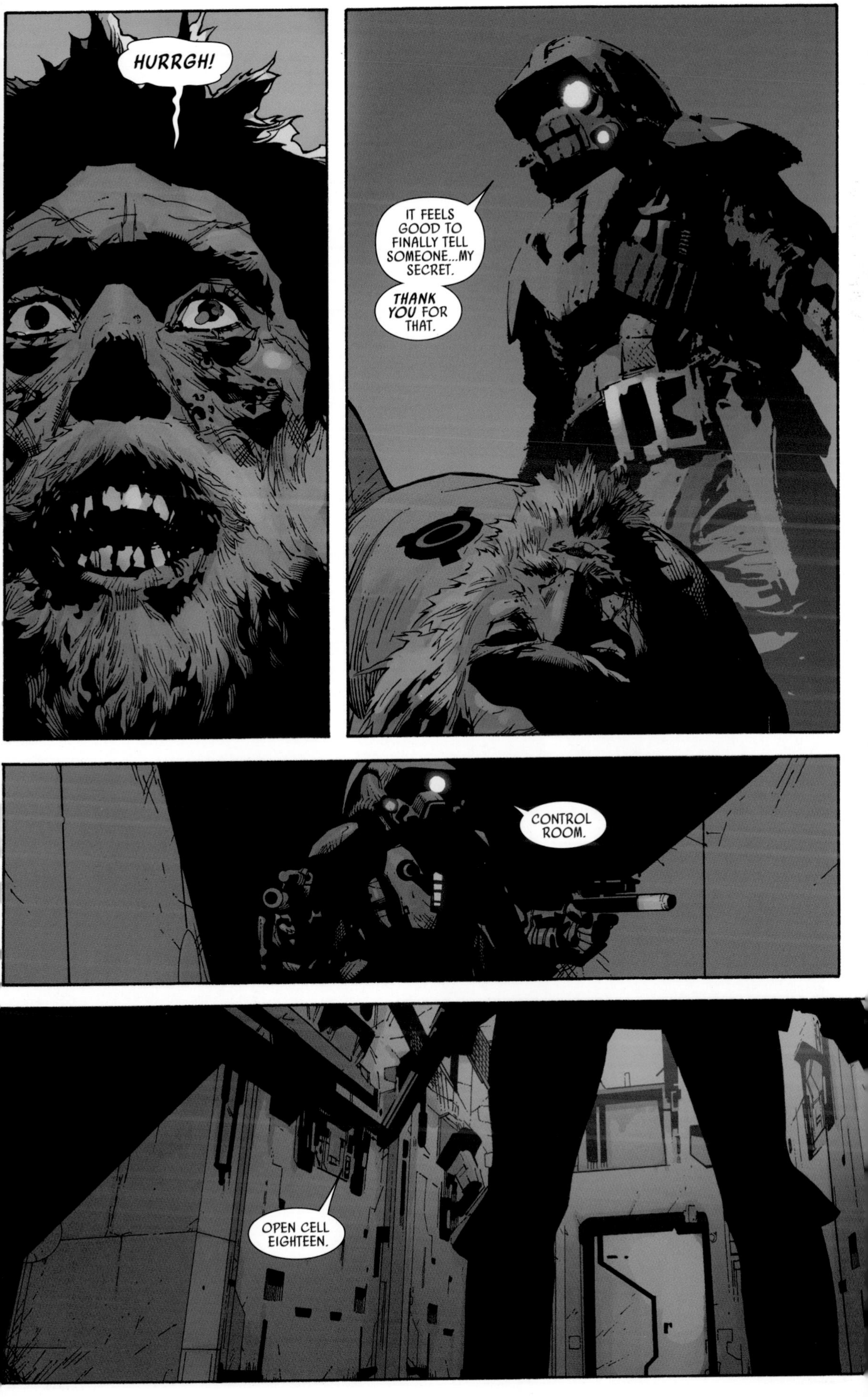
HURRGH!
IT FEELS GOOD TO FINALLY TELL SOMEONE...MY SECRET.
THANK YOU FOR THAT.
CONTROL ROOM.
OPEN CELL EIGHTEEN.

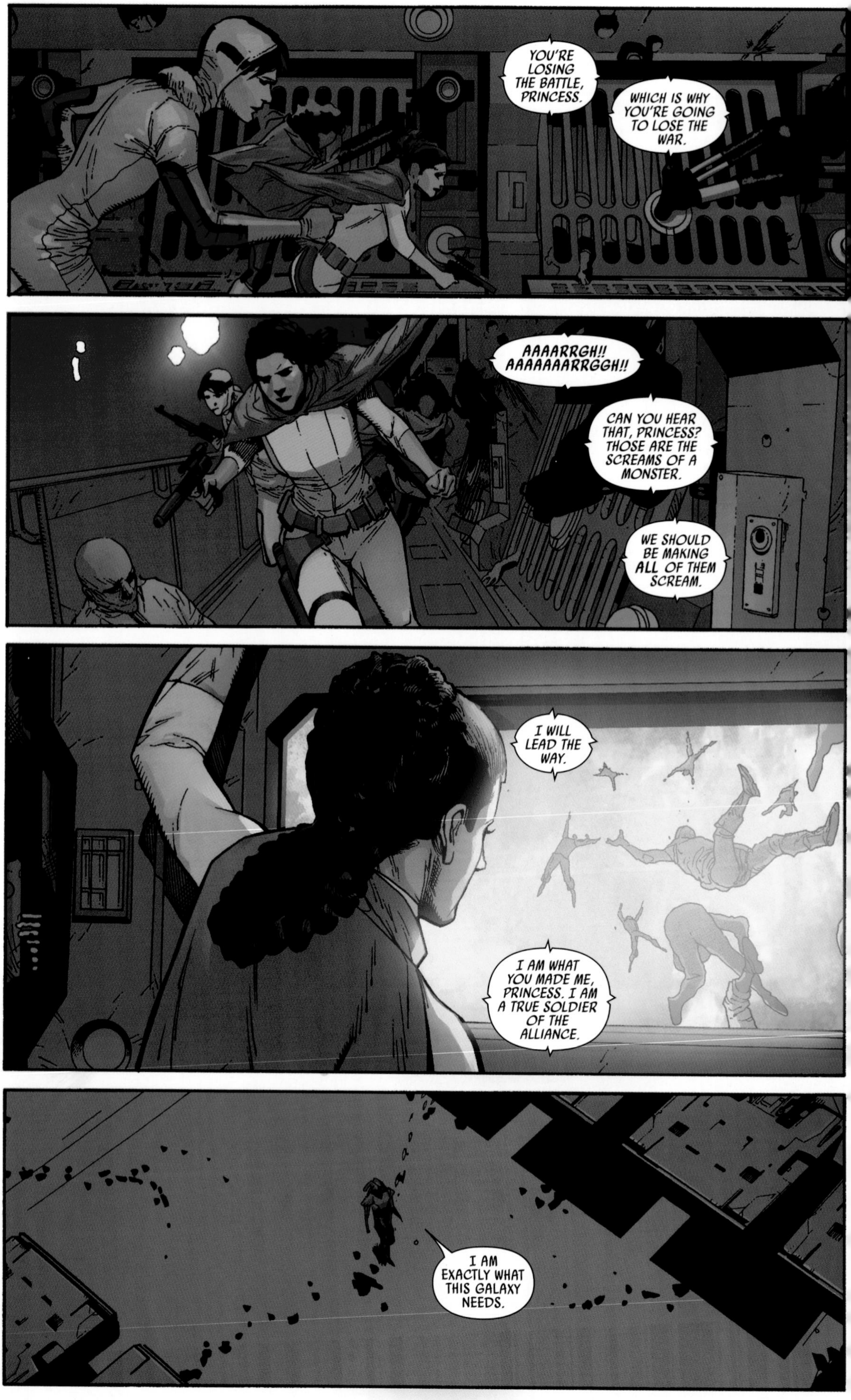
YOU'RE LOSING THE BATTLE, PRINCESS.
WHICH IS WHY YOU'RE GOING TO LOSE THE WAR.
AAAARRGH!! AAAAAAARRGGH!!
CAN YOU HEAR THAT, PRINCESS? THOSE ARE THE SCREAMS OF A MONSTER.
WE SHOULD BE MAKING ALL OF THEM SCREAM.
I WILL LEAD THE WAY.
I AM WHAT YOU MADE ME, PRINCESS. I AM A TRUE SOLDIER OF THE ALLIANCE.
I AM EXACTLY WHAT THIS GALAXY NEEDS.

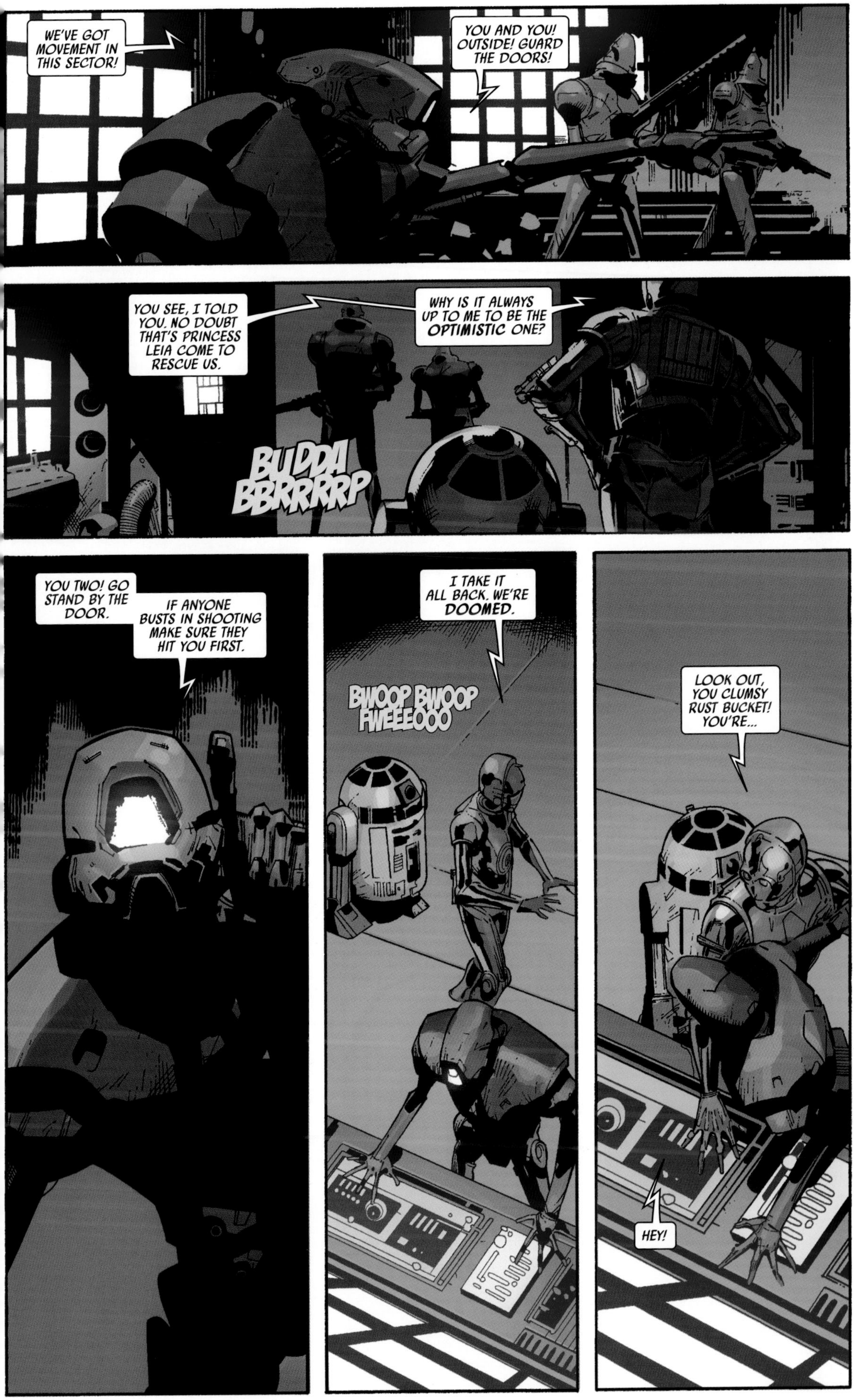
WE'VE GOT MOVEMENT IN THIS SECTOR!
YOU AND YOU! OUTSIDE! GUARD THE DOORS!
YOU SEE, I TOLD YOU. NO DOUBT THAT'S PRINCESS LEIA COME TO RESCUE US.
WHY IS IT ALWAYS UP TO ME TO BE THE OPTIMISTIC ONE?
BUDDA BBRRRRP
YOU TWO! GO STAND BY THE DOOR.
IF ANYONE BUSTS IN SHOOTING MAKE SURE THEY HIT YOU FIRST.
I TAKE IT ALL BACK. WE'RE DOOMED.
BWOOP BWOOP FWEEEOOO
LOOK OUT, YOU CLUMSY RUST BUCKET! YOU'RE...
HEY!

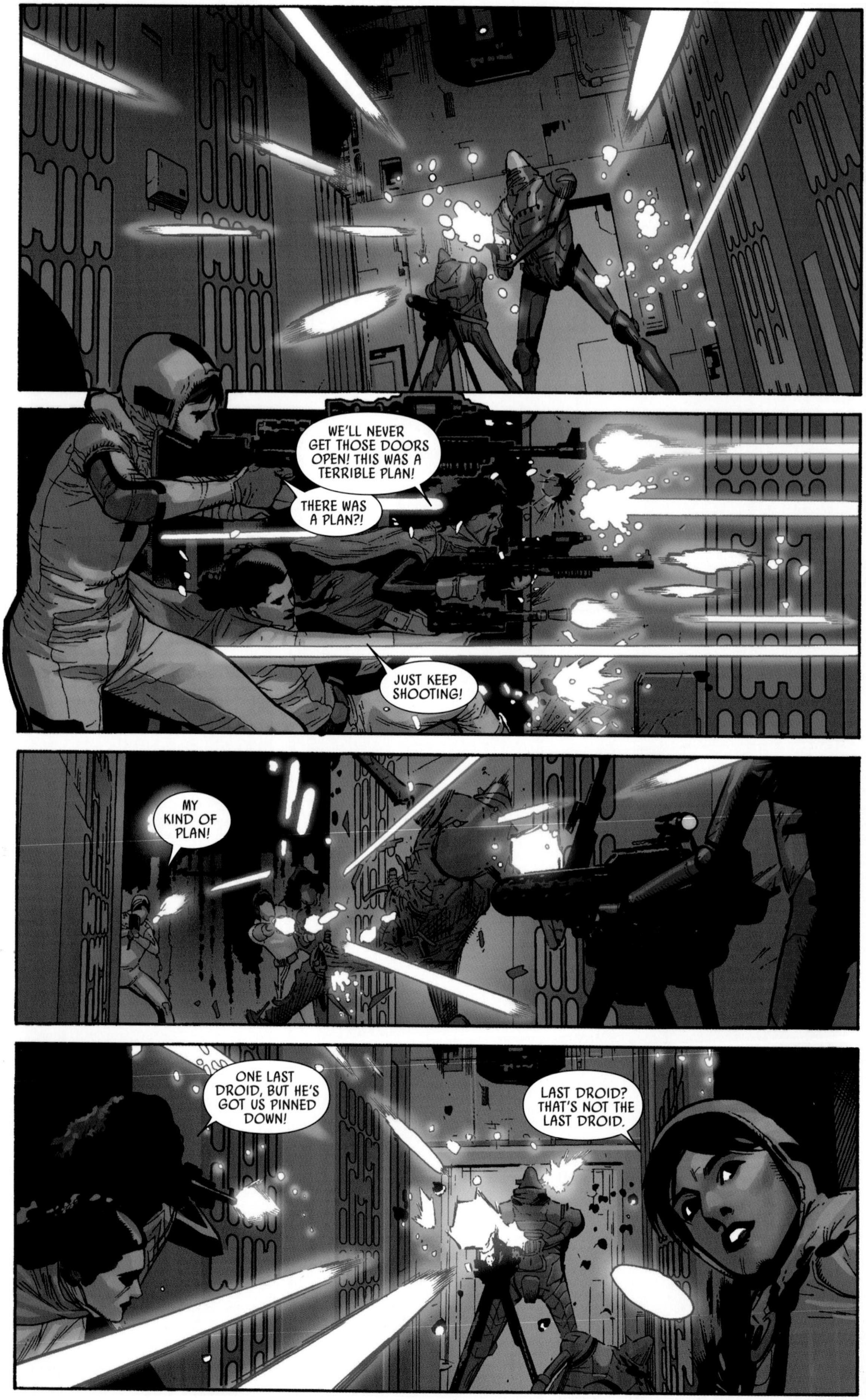
WE'LL NEVER GET THOSE DOORS OPEN! THIS WAS A TERRIBLE PLAN!
THERE WAS A PLAN?!
JUST KEEP SHOOTING!
MY KIND OF PLAN!
ONE LAST DROID, BUT HE'S GOT US PINNED DOWN!
LAST DROID? THAT'S NOT THE LAST DROID.

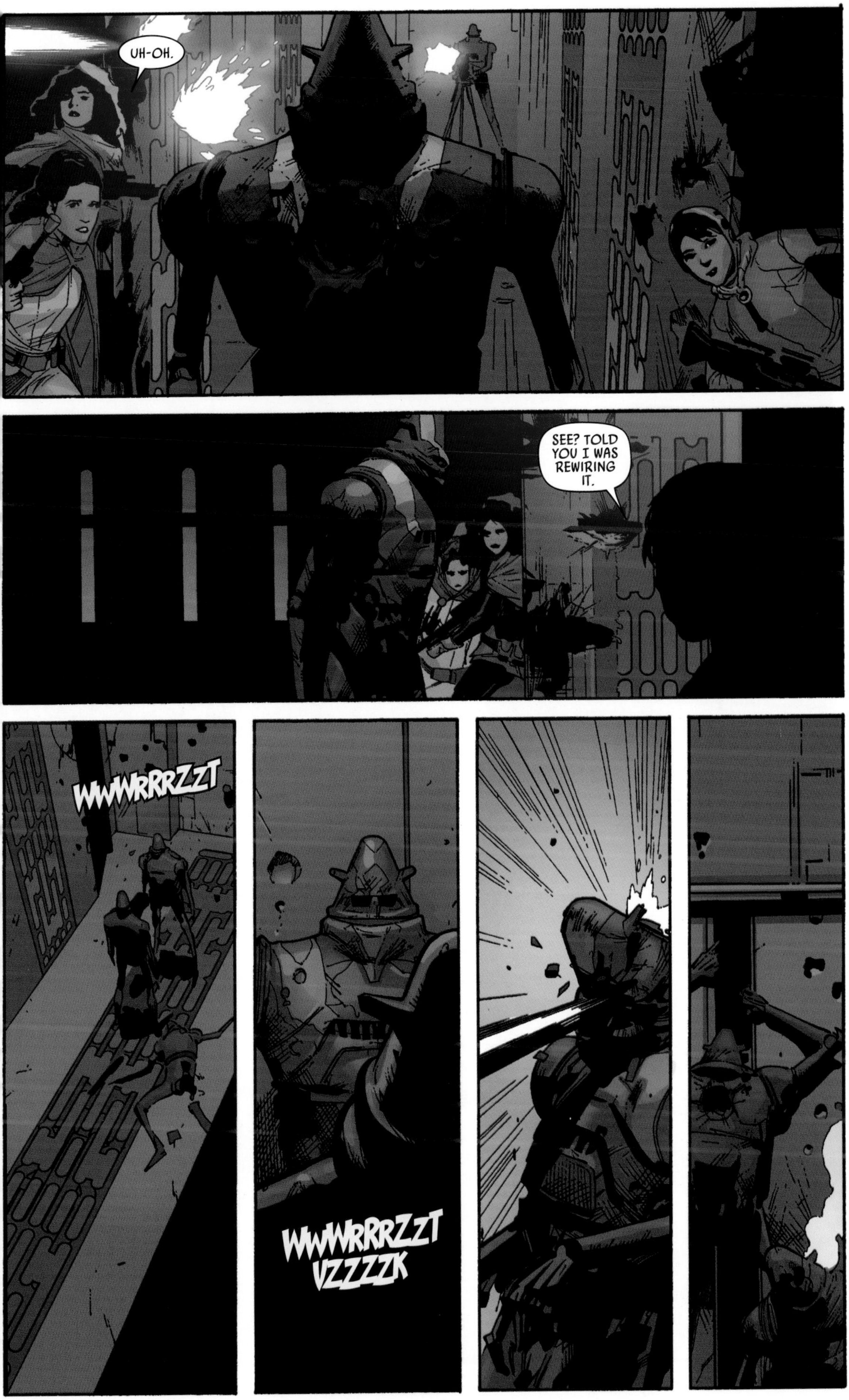
UH-OH.
SEE? TOLD YOU I WAS REWIRING IT.
WWWRRRZZT
WWWRRRZZT
VZZZZK

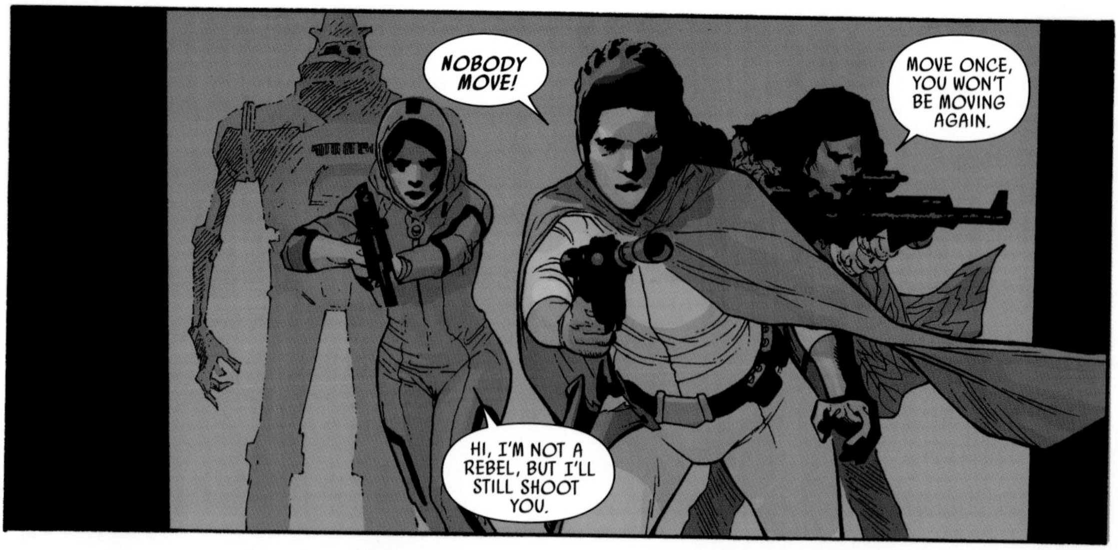
NOBODY MOVE!
MOVE ONCE, YOU WON'T BE MOVING AGAIN.
HI, I'M NOT A REBEL, BUT I'LL STILL SHOOT YOU.

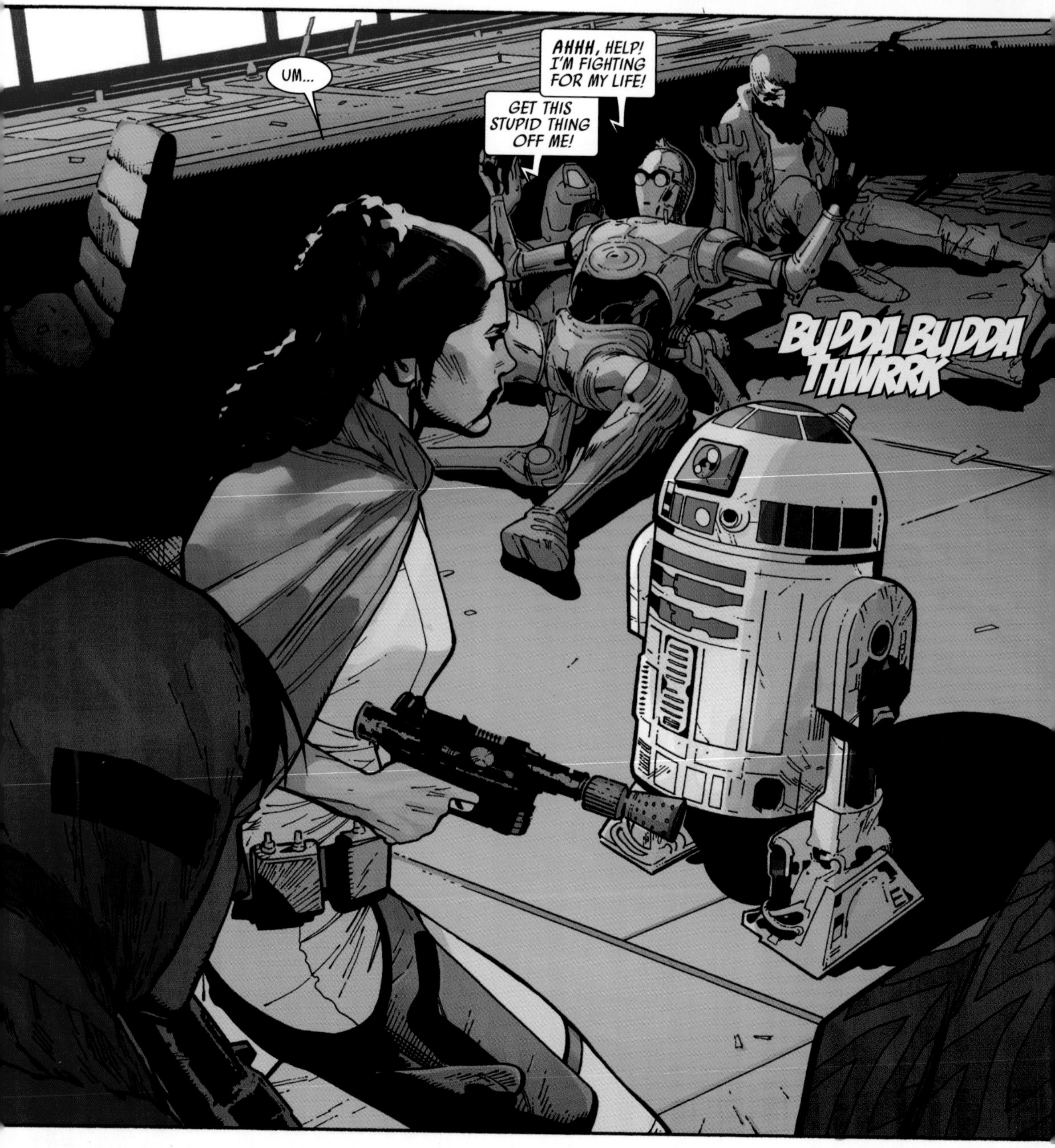
UM...
AHHH, HELP! I'M FIGHTING FOR MY LIFE!
GET THIS STUPID THING OFF ME!
BUDDA BUDDA THWRRK

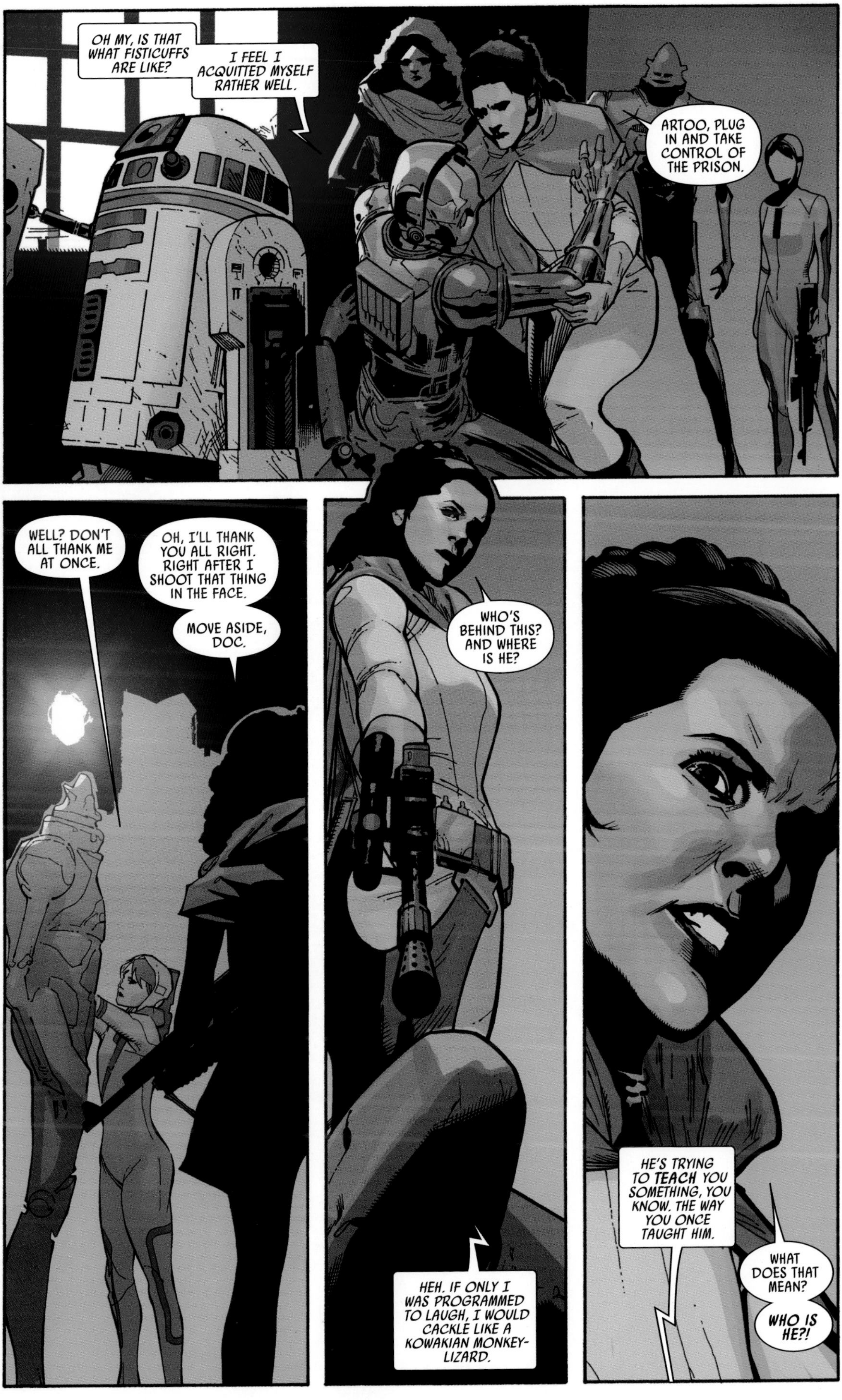
OH MY, IS THAT WHAT FISTICUFFS ARE LIKE?
I FEEL I ACQUITTED MYSELF RATHER WELL.
ARTOO, PLUG IN AND TAKE CONTROL OF THE PRISON.
WELL? DON'T ALL THANK ME AT ONCE.
OH, I'LL THANK YOU ALL RIGHT. RIGHT AFTER I SHOOT THAT THING IN THE FACE.
MOVE ASIDE, DOC.
WHO'S BEHIND THIS? AND WHERE IS HE?
HEH. IF ONLY I WAS PROGRAMMED TO LAUGH, I WOULD CACKLE LIKE A KOWAKIAN MONKEY-LIZARD.
HE'S TRYING TO TEACH YOU SOMETHING, YOU KNOW. THE WAY YOU ONCE TAUGHT HIM.
WHAT DOES THAT MEAN?
WHO IS HE?!

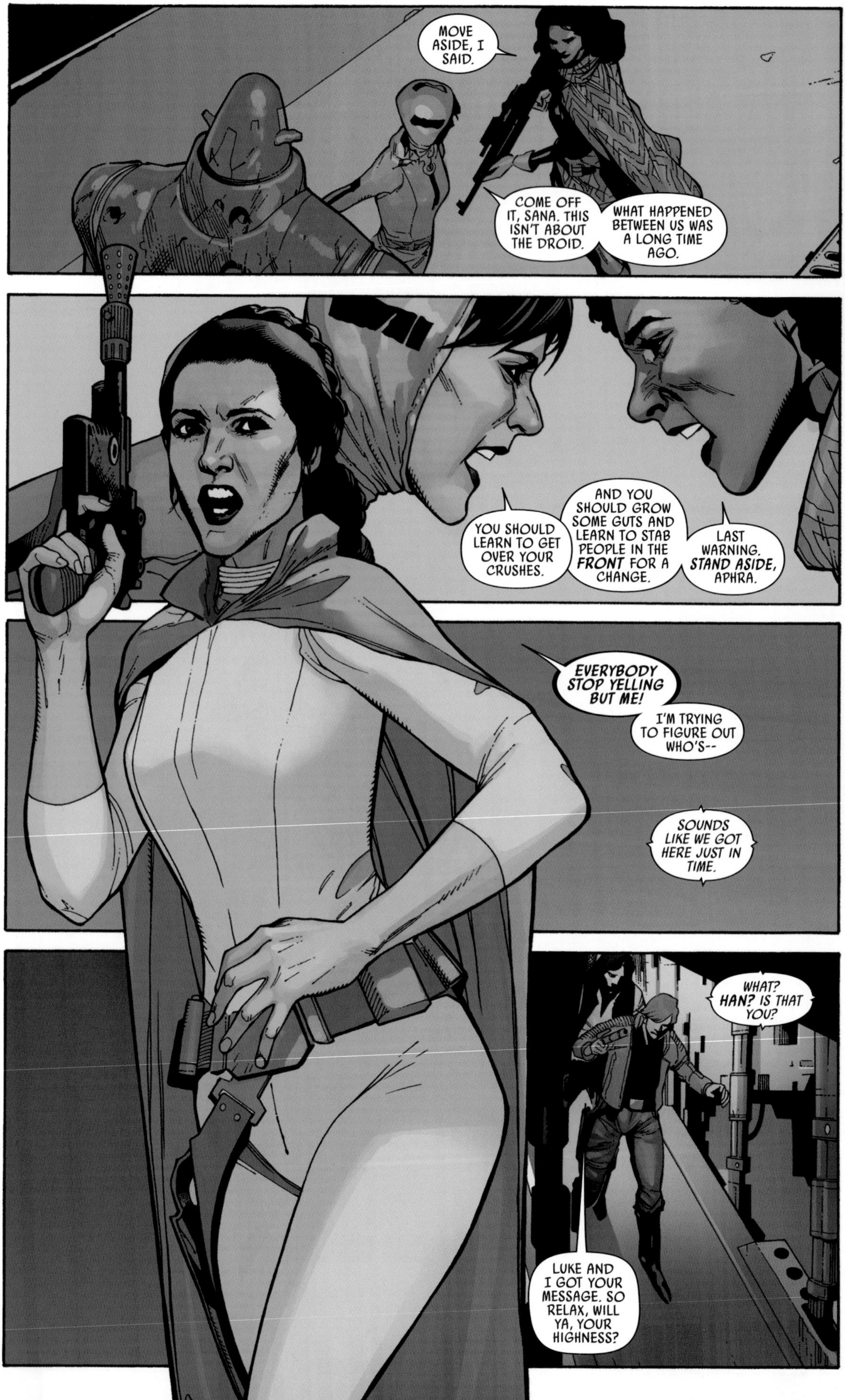
MOVE ASIDE, I SAID.
COME OFF IT, SANA. THIS ISN'T ABOUT THE DROID.
WHAT HAPPENED BETWEEN US WAS A LONG TIME AGO.
YOU SHOULD LEARN TO GET OVER YOUR CRUSHES.
AND YOU SHOULD GROW SOME GUTS AND LEARN TO STAB PEOPLE IN THE FRONT FOR A CHANGE.
LAST WARNING. STAND ASIDE, APHRA.
EVERYBODY STOP YELLING BUT ME!
I'M TRYING TO FIGURE OUT WHO'S--
SOUNDS LIKE WE GOT HERE JUST IN TIME.
WHAT? HAN? IS THAT YOU?
LUKE AND I GOT YOUR MESSAGE. SO RELAX, WILL YA, YOUR HIGHNESS?

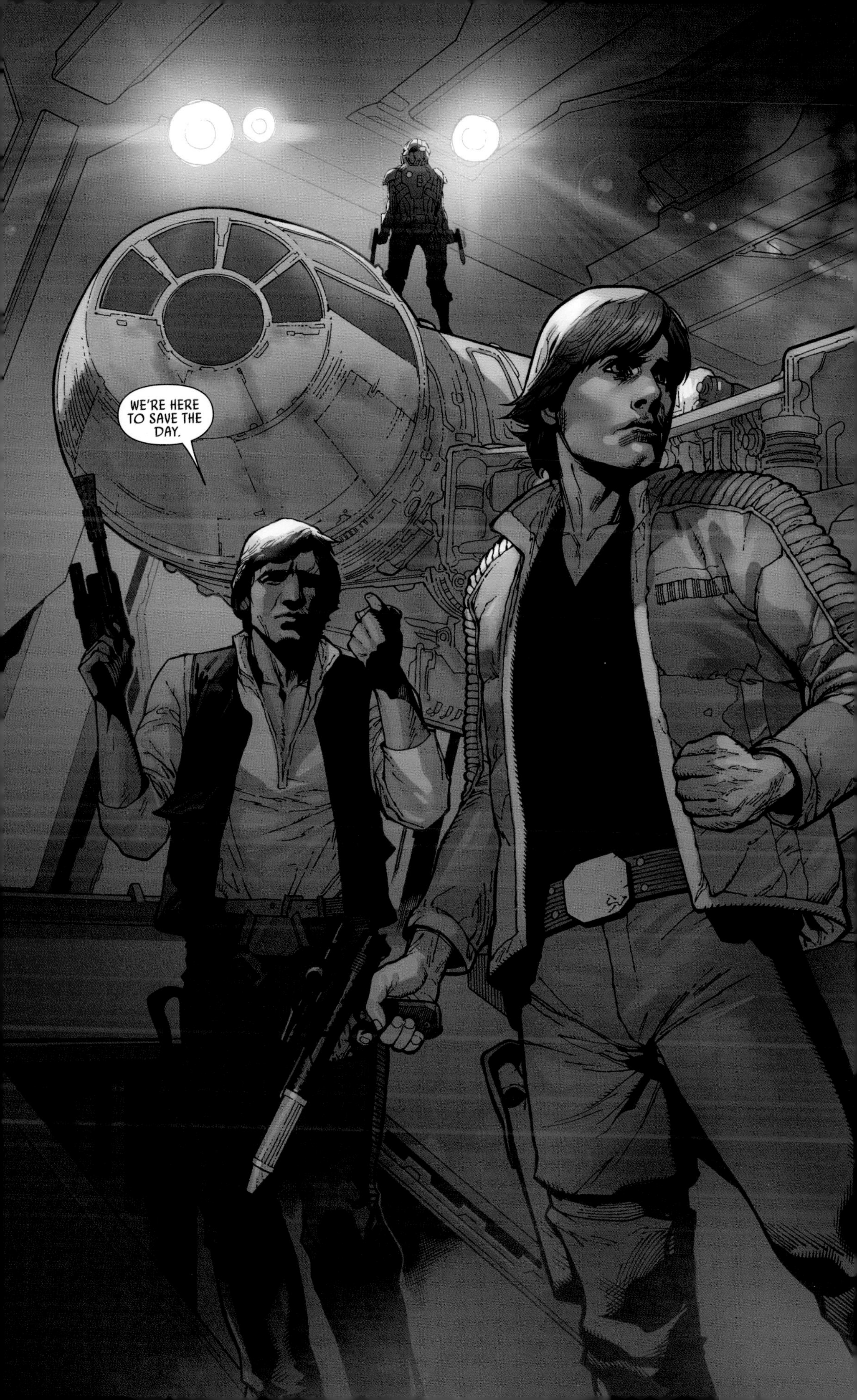
WE'RE HERE TO SAVE THE DAY.

STAR WARS™

REBEL JAIL

COLLECT THEM ALL!

Set of 5 Hardcover Books ISBN: 978-1-5321-4140-9

STAR WARS
STAR WARS
REBEL JAIL: VOLUME 1
AARON MAYHEW

Hardcover Book ISBN
978-1-5321-4141-6

STAR WARS
STAR WARS
REBEL JAIL: VOLUME 2
AARON YU ALANGUILAN GHO

Hardcover Book ISBN
978-1-5321-4142-3

STAR WARS
STAR WARS
REBEL JAIL: VOLUME 3
AARON YU GHO

Hardcover Book ISBN
978-1-5321-4143-0

STAR WARS
STAR WARS
REBEL JAIL: VOLUME 4
AARON YU ALANGUILAN GHO

Hardcover Book ISBN
978-1-5321-4144-7

STAR WARS
STAR WARS
REBEL JAIL: VOLUME 5
AARON YU ALANGUILAN GHO TARTAGLIA

Hardcover Book ISBN
978-1-5321-4145-4

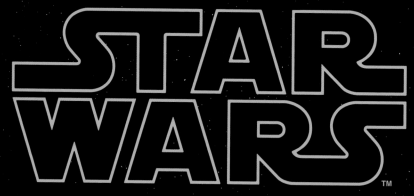

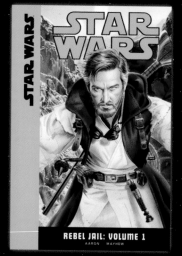

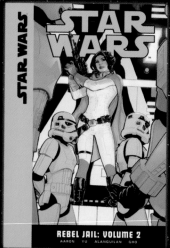

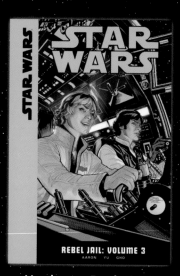

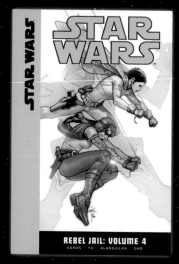

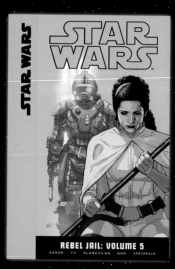